Sophie's New School

written by Kathy Lampert

illustrated by Melissa Bailey

Dear Mrs Morrison and her class !!

Have fun at school !

Love from Sophie's mommy - Kathy Lampert

For Sophie,
who inspired this book.

For Emma,
who inspires me to be a better person.

And for Marc,
who lets me be inspired.

I wake up in bed feeling comfy and warm.
Today's Monday.
Mommy says it's time to go to school.
I don't want to go!

Home is cozy and safe.
Mommy and I hug each other a lot.
Some days the whole house smells like cookies.

I say to Mommy, "Today's not really the day
and I'm really not old enough yet.
I'll just stay home with you, okay?"

Mommy says, "Today's the day, Honey.
Why would you want to stay home with me
when you can have fun at school?"

Mommy and I walk into my classroom together.
My teacher looks nice.
She says, "Hello, I'm Mrs. Snowman."
Her name is funny and I try to smile.

But I don't know what I'm supposed to say
and suddenly I feel shy and scared.
Now I don't feel like a very big girl at all.
And I don't feel cozy. And I don't feel safe.

So I try to be very brave instead.
I say, loud and clear so Mommy will be sure to listen,
"Mommy, can we please go home now?
I will try again another day."

Mommy says, "No, Honey, today is the day.
School is fun, you'll see."
Mommy hugs me and leaves.
I cry. A lot.

"Do you want to sit on my lap?"
asks Mrs. Snowman, and I nod my head yes.
I don't feel safe yet, but I do feel a bit cozy.

Mrs. Snowman doesn't feel like Mommy.
But she feels good.
And she knows how to give good hugs.

On the playground I make a friend.
She's very pretty and very nice.
She likes me and wants to play with me!

I really like being with my new friend.
Maybe tomorrow I'll ask her name.
IF I come back.

It's Tuesday morning.
I wake up in my warm snuggly bed.
Mommy says that it's time to go to school.

I say, "Again???
Mommy, today's not the day.
I went yesterday."

I wiggle under my blanket and cover my head.
Mommy says, "Mrs. Snowman will miss you
if you're not there."

I think she might be right.

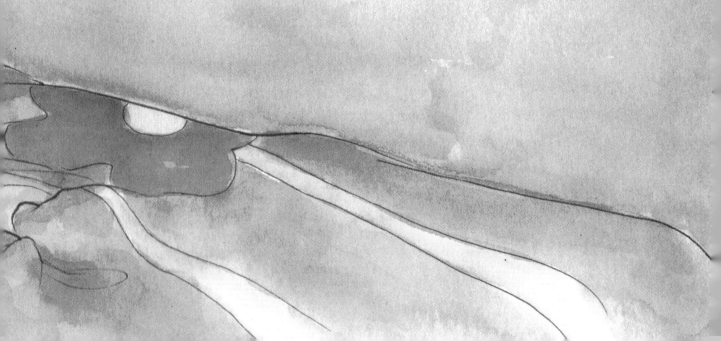

And I remember I have a friend at school.
Maybe I'll get out of bed.

Okay, I say to myself,
I'll try school **one** more time.

We walk into class, and I see Mrs. Snowman.
She smiles at me and says, "Hello Sophie.
I'm so glad you came back!"
And she really *does* look happy to see me.

Mommy kisses me goodbye.
It feels funny watching Mommy leave,
but I'm not crying!
I want to, but only a little bit.

Mrs. Snowman walks me over to my friend.
That was exactly what I wanted her to do!
I think, Mrs. Snowman, you did the right thing!

Mrs. Snowman says to me,
"Sophie, do you remember Brooke?
You played together yesterday."

The nice and pretty girl pats the swing,
and I sit right next to her.

My friend's name is Brooke,
and it is so fun to swing together!

Now I feel cozy and safe.
I think today will be the best day **ever**!

It's time to go home,
and I'm waiting outside with my coat on.

Mommy comes to pick me up, and I run to her.
I feel so happy!

Mommy hugs me and I say,
"Mommy, I had SO much fun today,
and I *really* like my new school!"

Mommy says, "Oh Sophie, I'm so delighted
to hear that. And I'm so *proud* of you!"

And I'm proud of me too.

I LOVE SCHOOL!

Made in the USA
Charleston, SC
22 August 2013